MURDER IN SHADES OF YELLOW

A DS Charlie Rees Novella

RIPLEY HAYES

Copyright © 2023 by Ripley Hayes

All rights reserved.

No part of this book may be reproduced in any form or by any electronic or mechanical means, including information storage and retrieval systems, without written permission from the author, except for the use of brief quotations in a book review.

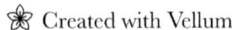 Created with Vellum

This one is for Lou, who made all the big decisions.

Foreword

This novella was produced as a freebie for subscribers to my newsletter. You may recognise Charlie Rees from the Daniel Owen books, but it's time for him to stand on his own two feet. Charlie's next book will be available in Spring 2023, and you can pre-order it here.
Murder in Shades of Blue and Green

Chapter 1

At first Charlie thought the screams were part of his dreams. After a night of booze, dancing and sex, who knew what was real? He felt the hot body half lying on his own, making him uncomfortable with sweat. He rolled to find coolness and return to sleep. But the screams continued. He ignored them. They were interspersed with a stream of hysterical Spanish, far beyond his ability to translate. The noise hurt his head. He was dehydrated and sore. Everything was sore. His head ached. And there was screaming. Charlie groaned and opened his eyes. His companion just groaned.

Then Charlie heard a word he understood only too well. "Policia! Policia!"

He scrambled from underneath the tangled sheets and into his jeans and last night's T-shirt. On the other side of the bed, his companion was doing the same, with the same urgency and focus. They almost collided at the door.

"Stay here," José Maria said, in heavily accented English. "I'm a police officer."

"So am I," Charlie said.

José Maria froze, his holding the door handle, brown skin

against the brushed steel. Then he gave a sharp nod, and opened the door. Charlie grabbed the key card from its slot. Across the tiled hall, a short, dyed-blonde woman in the hotel uniform of beige and navy blue stood in front of an open doorway with one hand on her cleaning trolley and the other clutching at her neck. And screamed. And screamed.

IT WAS the third day of a holiday Charlie hadn't wanted to take. His boss had insisted, citing the black rings round Charlie's eyes, his pasty skin and the ever-increasing workload.

"Nobody ever died from taking a holiday, DS Rees. The supply of crime won't be drying up anytime soon. Go home, book somewhere warm and pack your bag. That's an order."

He'd done as he was told, paid his money and a day later smiled at the hen party seated near him on the budget airline flight to Lanzarote. If they wanted to start drinking champagne at eleven in the morning, who was he to object? But he wasn't sorry they weren't in his hotel. If he had to take this trip, he wanted to sleep for as much of it as possible, and those girls made a lot of noise.

The hotel had been a surprise. He'd chosen almost at random, only partly guided by reviews or price. Faced with pages of pictures of sunlight glinting on impossibly blue swimming pools, he'd picked the travel company's recommendation just to get it done. The hotel was large and modern. His 'junior suite' turned out to be a big room with its own private terrace, bathroom and comfortable couch and a bigger TV than he had at home. To turn the lights on Charlie had to put his key card in a slot by the door, which he only discovered after fruitlessly bashing switches until he saw the green light winking on the wall and made the connection. The suites were arranged in clusters of four, each suite facing outwards for privacy, with its own little terrace. A small internal hallway provided keycard access to the suites.

Windows revealed palm trees, thick hedges and bushes with bright pink and orange flowers. In January. The air smelled of rosemary and pine. Everything was spotless, from the padded sun beds around the pools to the brick paths where not a dead leaf was left to lie. He still planned to spend his time sleeping, but he would be sleeping in beautiful surroundings.

He slept on and off for most of the first day, emerging only to eat from the buffet. On the second day, he woke refreshed enough to wander around the hotel grounds, wondering at the other guests. Mostly retired couples, he thought, men with terrible haircuts and dreadful shirts failing to conceal their bulging bellies. Their wives made more of an effort, with wildly patterned floaty garments. He resolved not to judge, even as he marvelled at their sipping cocktails by the pool at ten am. These people were entitled to holidays too. At lunch, he found himself a quiet corner, and settled down for some more people-watching. He saw there were families with children too young for school, a few young couples and a few singles like him. But most of the clientele were variations on the theme of 'if the booze is included, I'm making the best of it'.

After lunch he took his book to a sun bed by the pool, noting that Lee Child's works appeared on many of the sun beds, including his own. He imagined Jack Reacher's reaction to the acres of flabby flesh on display and hid a smile.

It's a good job I didn't come looking for romance. Or even a quick fuck.

He smiled to himself again, because who didn't go on holiday to the sunshine without the faint hope of meeting someone tasty? Then he saw the lifeguard: tall, dark skinned, with tattoos making sleeves on both arms. Big brown eyes looked out from under a blindingly white baseball cap matching the white T shirt with SOS printed in red letters on the front. Tight black shorts finished the outfit. Charlie was doing his best not to stare, when a slightly camp voice in his ear whispered, "He's not for us, sweetie."

Charlie jerked in surprise, dropping his book. He found himself looking into a pair of dark sunglasses — designer sunglasses — adorning a tanned face, with good skin and a perfectly trimmed goatee. His gaydar had pinged at the sound of the voice, and it pinged again, loudly.

"Pat," said the man, "and this is my hubby, Gray. Hi."

Gray looked over Pat's shoulder at another well-groomed, tanned face, this one clean shaven.

"I told you," Pat said to his husband.

Gray sighed. "Ignore him," he said with a smile. "Pat here assumes that anyone with a properly ironed shirt and shorts that fit must be gay."

"He was ogling Rafael, and he's wearing Pride Vans on his feet. Tell me I'm not wrong, sweetie." This last to Charlie, who laughed.

"I'm Charlie, pleased to meet you both, and no, you're not wrong."

"Then Gray can go and get the drinks," Pat said. "Specials all round. It's included after all." He winked.

Over the course of several specials, Pat and Gray entertained Charlie with the *inside goss* about the hotel, where the couple had been coming *for years, sweetie,* about Rafael the lifeguard "women only, and lots of them. But he's slowed down a bit. We think he's got a girlfriend."

"That's as maybe but he was all over that woman who does the excursions yesterday," Gray interrupted with a mock shudder. "I had to look away."

The specials segued into a couple of bottles of wine over dinner, until when Pat told them they were all going dancing, Charlie went to get changed in a contented haze. The club was busy, but not so busy that Charlie didn't start swapping meaningful glances with a man even sexier than the lifeguard. A couple more drinks topped up the haze of contentment and sealed the deal with José Maria. The haze lasted through hours of dancing, even more drinks and a taxi ride back to the hotel. It lasted through some excellent sex, and helped him ignore the pale band of skin around José Maria's ring finger. In fact, it lasted until the screams woke him up.

Chapter 2

José Maria looked into the room, and Charlie saw his skin pale and watched him swallow convulsively as if trying not to throw up. He urged the screaming woman to move herself and her cleaning trolley away from the door, murmuring to her in Spanish. He caught Charlie's eye.

"Could you take her outside to sit down?" José Maria asked, "And get my cell phone?"

Charlie nodded and stepped forward to grasp the housekeeper's arm. She was tiny, and her arms were as thin as a bird's. José Maria's tall body blocked the doorway, but Charlie didn't need to see inside to know that it was bad. He could smell the blood.

The housekeeper's name tag read 'Marita'. Charlie used it, along with his limited Spanish to try to calm her down. She kept repeating the Spanish words for *I saw, I saw*, over and over. What she had seen would stay with her in nightmares for a long time, Charlie thought. He helped her to sit on the low wall of black lava chunks outside the main door, patting her arm. She was sobbing now, tears streaming down her face, dampening her hair and clothes. Her dyed blonde hair had been braided tightly against her head, but the braids were coming loose in her distress.

"I'll be right back," he said, patting her shoulder again. Then he sprinted back to his room, grabbed the phone from the bedside table and came to a dead stop. José Maria was standing on the pale tiles in the hallway looking down at his bare feet. There was a trail of bloody footprints between where he stood and the open door.

"Fuck," he said, and reached for the phone Charlie held out to him.

CHARLIE STEPPED ROUND the bloody prints, the tiles cool and hard against his own bare feet. He looked into the room, and understood José Maria's reaction. Blood. Blood everywhere. Soaking the white bedcovers, splashed on the patterned headboard, blood on the bedside table, coating a phone, a wallet and a hotel keycard, blood in Rorschach blots on the floor. A bloody towel lay on the tiles like a doormat. In the middle of it all, on the bed, the body of a naked man, both arms covered in tattoos. And blood.

The body had slumped sideways in a macabre simulation of the recovery position. There would be no recovery from this. Charlie's gaze focussed on the man's toes, possibly the only part of him not covered in blood. The nails were clean and neatly trimmed. Above the nails, soft-looking dark hair curled over. A long knife lay by his side, blade and handle alike smeared brown. The murder weapon, because this could only be murder.

BEHIND HIM, Charlie could hear José Maria shouting into his phone. With a final "valé" the call ended.

"Charlie," José Maria said, and let his breath out in a long sigh.

"It's the lifeguard, isn't it? The dead man," Charlie said.

José Maria shrugged. "My colleagues are coming. My boss. Detectives. CSIs. The doctor. It will be busy. You will have to say what you saw."

"I know," Charlie said. "I'm a detective. At home."

And one of the things I've detected is that you're almost certainly married and there's going to be some explaining to do about why you were here.

José Maria nodded as if he had understood Charlie's thoughts, but all he said was "we should get dressed before they get here. I want to wash my feet." He looked down at his feet. No blood was visible, but the blood on the floor could only have come from José Maria's feet. Charlie was thankful that he hadn't stepped into the room with his own bare feet.

"Dressed. Good idea." Then. "José Maria. Is this going to be embarrassing for you? Being here I mean. Does your wife know?"

José Maria smiled a thin smile. "Not yet. It is a pleasure still to come."

WITH A BLAST of sirens and a swirl of blue lights, the familiar circus arrived. Charlie had no difficulty recognising the pathologist, the senior detective and the white-suited scenes-of-crime investigators. Officers put up crime scene tape, escorted Charlie back to his room, and thoroughly and efficiently searched it while he watched. Eventually a short grey-haired man in a dark suit entered and gestured to the seating area. From the deference shown by the other officers, Charlie deduced that this was the man in charge.

"Señor Rees," he said, in an American accent. Charlie supposed his English teacher was from the USA. He nodded. "Señor Rees. Please tell me everything that you did since yesterday, say from dinner time onwards."

"How do you know who I am?" Charlie asked.

His only answer was a shrug and a smile.

"Why from dinner time? This man was killed much later than that."

Another shrug. Another smile.

Charlie wanted to return the shrug. But he'd been a policeman for long enough to know it would be pointless. So he described the drinks by the pool, the dinner and the club. Then he hesitated. José Maria had made his own decisions, was probably lying to his wife, but Charlie didn't want him in any deeper water than he could help. He, Charlie worked for a gay man, and there was still homophobia around the office. He had no idea how José Maria's boss would react to discovering that one of his officers had spent the night in another man's bed.

"You picked Perez up in the club, and the two of you came back here for sex. Yes?"

For a moment, Charlie wondered who 'Pérez' could be. He blushed.

"He was with you all night?"

"José Maria? Yes. Marita's screams woke us up."

"Can you be sure about that? Are you certain that Pérez wasn't already awake?"

He was lying on top of me, snoring. But, hey, if there's a gay man to blame, let's do it.

"I think I would have noticed if he got up to go and murder someone." Charlie said firmly.

All he got in return was another shrug and smile.

Chapter 3

They were interrupted by shouting. Cries of "Mama! Mama!" in a high-pitched feminine voice, and the deeper voices of men angry at being ignored. All the voices got louder until José Maria's boss muttered a curse and stood up, forcing the chair backwards against the wall.

"¿Qué pasa?" he roared and slammed his way out of the room. Charlie followed, quietly, wanting to know, but not wanting to be seen and sent away. He was careful to remove the key card from its slot by the door; second nature after only two days.

A young woman in a neat navy skirt and jacket was being restrained by a uniformed officer in the doorway to the suite of rooms. The silk scarf around her neck had become disordered, and wisps of hair had escaped from her ponytail. Charlie thought she had been a well-put-together package when she arrived for work — now, not so much. On the floor lay a clipboard bearing the word "Excursions" in large letters. Every time the officer's grip on her arms eased, she began to gesticulate wildly, still shouting "Mama! ¿Donde es mi madre?" Charlie had enough Spanish to translate *where is my mother?* But once José Maria's boss appeared, all the officers began talking at once and Charlie lost track.

The senior detective raised his hand and silence fell. When he began to speak, he did so slowly enough for Charlie to follow.

"Who is this woman?"

"Inspector Jefe, she is the daughter of the worker who found the body."

"Inspector Jefe, she works at the hotel."

Finally José Maria's boss addressed the woman directly. "Señora, you must leave. Your mother is well." He gave her a card, and waved her away. To Charlie's surprise, she went.

The chief inspector turned round and caught sight of Charlie. His brows drew together and there was no sign of the smile.

"This is a crime scene, Señor Rees. My officer will arrange for you to have a different room so you can continue with your holiday." His tone did not allow for argument. "Please understand that this is a law-abiding island. There is no need for you to be concerned."

That's me told.

Charlie was allowed to collect his few things, packing them quickly in his carry-on suitcase. He ignored the uniformed officer's look of disdain as he picked the lube and condom packets from the floor by the bed. Screw him. The officer escorted him back to the reception desk, where the receptionist consulted their computer and a colleague before asking for Charlie's key card, putting it into a machine pressing some keys and returning it to him with a smile.

"Please accept our apologies for this change. There will be no charge for your stay with us."

CHARLIE'S new room was identical to the old one. He showered and dressed in clean clothes. It was lunchtime. He chose the smaller pool bar for a sandwich and a beer, though in truth he would have preferred a nap. Siesta afterwards, he thought. He felt that he ought to take a swim, or use the hotel gym, but the drinking the night before and the shock of waking to find a murder had left him lethargic. He was supposed to be having a break. This was business as usual, except he wasn't allowed to *do* anything. The urge to question the staff around the pool where the dead man had worked, was strong; automatic and hard to ignore. But ignore it he would. *Holiday* he repeated silently as he sipped his beer and watched the sun dance on the water. Between the palm trees and white villas, the red-brown mountains loomed. Stark against the hard blue sky, they could only be volcanoes. Every wall and path was built from their lava, and the 'soil' was crushed black stone. Yet all the photographs Charlie had seen featured only swimming pools, white buildings, yellow sand and tropical greenery. The volcanoes were everywhere, but invisible to the tourist industry.

There was a cough and Charlie looked up to see one of the hotel staff.

"Mr Rees?" Charlie nodded.

"I have a note for you."

THE NOTE WAS WRITTEN in English, though the handwriting was subtly different from the handwriting taught in British schools. Something about the big loops, maybe? It read:

CHARLIE,

Would you meet me at the bar by Playa Las Palmas at 1400? Out of the hotel, turn left, pass the Mirador and the Aquapark and then downhill to the beach. 5 minutes walk only.

José M^a (Perez)

Murder in Shades of Yellow

. . .

IT WAS ALREADY ALMOST TWO. It wasn't hard to list the reasons not to go. José Maria was a married man; the murder was none of his business, and he wanted to sleep. But Charlie was a detective. If they sawed through his bones when he was dead, the letters *I want to know what happened* would run through them like the name of a seaside resort through a stick of rock. Of course he would go. He finished his beer and made his way to the hotel entrance.

ONCE OUTSIDE THE HOTEL GROUNDS, the mountains were even more ubiquitous. Nothing grew on their steep slopes but more square, flat-roofed white buildings; new urbanisations creeping ever upwards. The beach itself was a sad example of the genre, especially to someone used to the beaches of Wales. Massive concrete blocks sheltered the tiny bay, keeping the little arc of sand from being swept into the Atlantic. A crowd of scuba divers-in-training made their way in and out of the water like oversized black beetles. An African man hawked patterned sarongs and beach mats. Some north European women sunbathed topless in the hot sun while Spanish families kept their sweaters on against the cold January temperatures.

The bar advertised cocktails, ice cream, and pizza. José Maria stood up in welcome and Charlie admired his long limbs and broad shoulders, now clad in clean, well-fitting jeans and a white shirt-sleeved shirt. Charlie guessed his age as early thirties, perhaps younger. He had the kind of open face that Charlie always found attractive — big eyes and a ready smile.

I bet he looks amazing in his uniform.
Shame about the married thing.

. . .

"THANK YOU FOR MEETING ME," José Maria said, once they both had glasses of beer. He looked nervous. "No one will say so, but that Rafael had it coming." He turned his gaze out to sea, where a line of scuba trainees were making their slow way back to the beach, weighed down by equipment.

"Rafael was the lifeguard? The man who was killed?"

"Sí. Lanzarote doesn't have murders, but if anyone ..."

"I heard he was promiscuous," Charlie said.

"Ha! He fucked anything that moved. I think he was fucking my wife."

What's sauce for the goose... Charlie didn't say, but José Maria blushed anyway. Blushing suited him.

"Hypocritical, yes? The thing is, by the time Carmela and I realised we didn't like each other, we had a child." His face softened. "Still, I thought she had better taste. Like I do." He winked at Charlie, managing to make it look cute rather than obnoxious.

Charlie wondered just how OK Carmela Perez really was with her husband's activities. Or if she even knew.

José Maria said: "I wanted to talk. One police officer to another. To give you the chance to talk. Like I say, Lanzarote doesn't have murder. I'm not allowed anywhere near the case. I'm not a detective, but I can't help wanting to know what happened ... maybe you do too?"

Words as seductive to Charlie's lizard brain as José Maria's smiles had been the night before.

Chapter 4

"Do your colleagues have any ideas?" Charlie asked.

José Maria looked down at his hands resting on the table.

"Yes. And one of them is me."

Without thinking, Charlie picked up one of the hands and squeezed it. "You have an alibi. From a policeman, a detective sergeant."

"Do I? Can you prove I didn't leave?" He shook his head. Then his brown eyes met Charlie's, and Charlie remembered the night before. Surely he would have woken if his companion had left the bed? And he would have been covered in blood. He said as much.

"They found latex gloves in the shower. A used shower cap. And blood. Whoever did it wore gloves and had a shower afterwards. Put towels on the floor to get to the door without standing in blood. There are no fingerprints except from the cleaner — Marita."

"Marita had every reason to be there."

José Maria nodded.

Charlie continued. "Do they know what Rafael was doing in the room? I mean, I can guess, but whose room was it?"

"It was no one's room. Empty ... my wife, Carmela, works

15

at the hotel …" he sighed. "Everyone here works at a hotel, and Carmela works at this one. On reception. She was working last night. That's why I … I knew she was busy, and our little one was with her mother …" José Maria went back to gazing out to sea while Charlie untangled his own thoughts.

"The reception staff would know which rooms were empty and could give Rafael a keycard. So he could meet someone. A guest maybe? No, they would have used the guest's room. So, a staff member."

He wondered whether the staff member had been Carmela herself, taking a break from her duties to sneak away for an encounter with the hot lifeguard, not realising that her own husband was in the room opposite … or perhaps Carmela had supplied the key and Rafael had used it to meet someone else …

"Do you know what the receptionists have told the police?" Charlie asked.

"Ha! Nothing. They are all saying nothing. Denying everything. If the hotel found anyone giving out keycards like that, they would be sacked."

"What about Carmela? Can't you ask her?"

"You think she is speaking to me? Oh, Charlie, I can tell you have never been married. She won't even let me through the door."

I live in a small town though. Where everyone knows everyone else's business.

"How did Marita know that room would need cleaning? Who told her it had been used?"

José Maria shook his head.

"Let me guess. Too upset to speak to the police? And frightened about losing her job."

José Maria nodded. "It is a mess."

They sat in silence, Charlie listening to the conversations around him — in Spanish, Dutch, German and all varieties of English. The bar was busy despite it being the siesta. Perhaps in a place like this, with so many visitors, the siesta didn't happen. A waiter passed them and raised his eyebrows.

"¿Mas?" he asked. *More?*

Charlie nodded, and a moment later, two more beers arrived. He was on holiday, and his companion was barred from his home and his job. Sitting in the sun and drinking beer made perfect sense.

"Who was Rafael's companion, do you think?" Charlie asked as the level dropped in the beer glasses.

José Maria shrugged. "Elisa? Marita's daughter. Maybe. I heard she was interested. A few weeks ago, I would have said Carmela. Who knows with Rafael? If they are pretty …"

"¿JOSÉ Maria? Why are you drinking beer at my bar when there's a murderer to catch?" The questions came from a man in black trousers, a white T-shirt and a battered and stained white apron. He slapped José Maria on the back and looked curiously at Charlie.

José Maria coughed, choking a little on his beer.

"Andres. This is my friend Charlie from the UK. Charlie, Andres who owns this bar. Also, my friend since we were boys." He looked at the bar owner. "I found Rafael's body. I was in the hotel. They won't let me work on it."

"You were in the hotel? Your wife works there. Why shouldn't you be there?" Andres looked puzzled for a moment, then said, "You were not with Carmela. You were with someone else."

Charlie kept quiet. This was José Maria's call.

"I was with Charlie," José Maria said, folding his arms across his chest, his chin jutting forward as if challenging his friend to object.

Andres simply shrugged. "OK. So you have an alibi. Good. Why were you out finding bodies instead of …?" He wriggled his eyebrows and grinned.

"The cleaner. You remember Elisa from school? Her mother. She opened the door and screamed. I was close by. Asleep. I shouldn't be talking about it."

"My friend, the entire island is talking about it," Andres said.

"And who does the entire island think did it?" José Maria asked.

Chapter 5

Two more beers down, and Charlie felt mellow and sleepy. The sun warmed his face, possibly too much for a pale-faced Celt. But a little reddened skin was a small price to pay for an afternoon by a beach and beers in good company. Under the table, José Maria had slipped his hand onto Charlie's thigh and was moving his fingers in a way that was giving Charlie ideas about what they could do next. Andres supplied them with chips and sandwiches to help soak up the beer, and then went back to work, leaving the two of them alone.

"Want to come back to the hotel?" Charlie asked.

"I have to be at work at eight, patrolling the streets," José Maria said, "but ... why not?"

Back in his room, Charlie tossed the keycard onto the table. They wouldn't need the overhead lights or the TV for what he had in mind. Soft light from the setting sun glowed through the voile curtains as they kicked their shoes off and fell on to the bed. By the time the outside lights came on, their clothes had joined the shoes on the floor. Some time later, Charlie felt himself drifting in to a post orgasmic doze.

This is a much better way to spend my holiday than finding dead bodies. But maybe a shower is called for.

CHARLIE MADE them both coffee after their showers, and curled up at one end of the sofa. José Maria leaned against him.

"It's a shame you're only here for a week," he said, "because this has been fun."

"Perhaps it's been fun *because* I'm going home in a few days." Charlie said, thinking that was probably true. If he got the chance to sleep with José Maria again before he went, he'd take it. If not, well, that's life and there would be no regrets.

"Was your friend Andres right, do you think, about Marita and Elisa?" he asked.

"Everything he said was true. Lots of talk about Marita when we were at school. How she wouldn't let Elisa out of her sight. No one knew who Elisa's father was, which was bad enough. Then there was a scandal when Marita went for one of the teachers with a knife. He'd given Elisa a bad mark. Marita disappeared afterwards. People told us kids that *Elisa is staying with her grandmother because her mama is unwell.* This was a conservative place away from the tourists — mental illness was shameful. Still is."

"So Marita is a ready scapegoat?"

José Maria nodded.

"Small place, long memories. I wasn't supposed to talk to Elisa when we were kids, as if it was her fault her mother was unmarried, or mentally ill."

"I'm guessing someone called José Maria has a religious family?"

"My mother goes to mass every morning. She prayed for years for me to become a priest. She promised God a million euros if I got a vocation. If she knew I was here …"

There was no need to finish the sentence.

"And Carmela? How does she feel about it?" Charlie caught himself. "Sorry, it's none of my business. Forget I asked. Policeman's habit." Charlie squeezed José Maria's shoulder. "Sorry," he said again.

"It's OK. I have to go to work." But it obviously wasn't OK.

WHEN JOSÉ MARIA HAD GONE, Charlie lay against the back of the sofa and reflected. Could the tiny chambermaid have stabbed Rafael because he had ill-treated Elisa? Was there even any evidence that Elisa had been ill-treated by Rafael or anyone else? She had certainly been hysterical when Charlie had seen her, but anyone would be, coming across Rafael's body unexpectedly. She had a history of violence, but that was a long time ago, even if the locals persisted in remembering. Whatever "the island" had decided, Charlie wasn't ready to convict Marita just yet. He looked at the time. Dinner.

He was pleased to see Pat and Gray tucking into plates of paella, a bottle of wine half empty on the table beside them.

"Come and join us!" Pat called.

Charlie helped himself to paella, and wine, ordering another bottle when the waiter came by.

"Did you hear?" Pat said excitedly. "One of the cleaning staff murdered Rafael the lifeguard!"

"Stabbed him," said Gray.

"Bought a huge knife from that big supermercardo by the marina. All caught on CCTV, of course. But she's gone on the run. The cops can't find her."

Charlie pasted the most neutral expression he could manage onto his face. "How do you know all this stuff?" he asked.

"We've been coming here for so long that we fade into the background," Pat said. "They were talking about it at the reception desk. One of the receptionists has a friend who works in the supermercado. No secrets in a place like this."

"The cleaner turns out to be the mother of our excursions lady," Gray said. "The one we told you was snogging Rafael."

"It's like an episode of Murder in Paradise," Pat said. "Luxury hotel, hidden passions, secrets and lies. It will turn out that the cleaner didn't do it after all." He sighed with contentment.

It really isn't. It's nothing like the TV. If Marita bought that knife, it probably was her.

"Of course Rafael had it coming," Pat continued.

"Because he slept around?" Charlie asked, interested that so many people thought Rafael deserved his fate.

"If sleeping around got people murdered, how many of us would be left? Don't answer that. No, sweetie, Rafael had it coming because he was a nasty little blackmailer."

Chapter 6

Gray choked on his wine. "Pat. Come on, I'd hardly call it *blackmail*."

"What would you call it, then?" Pat said.

"A damn cheek? Eye to the main chance?"

"Blackmail. Pure and simple. Pay up or I tell."

Charlie's eyes flicked from Pat to Gray and back again. He enjoyed the verbal ping-pong, but he wanted to know what had happened.

Gray let out a deep breath. "We'll let Charlie decide."

"Fine. He'll agree with me." Pat poured the last of the wine into their glasses. "And when he does, you can attract the waiter's attention for another."

"Done." Gray leaned forward and spoke in a confidential voice. "So, Pat and I have an open relationship. Sometimes we fuck other people. Not often …"

"Getting too old, sweetie," Pat interrupted. Gray gave him a dirty look.

"Like I say, not often. A couple of years ago there was a nice young man, and I went to his room for the siesta. Good body, but I prefer someone who knows what they're doing."

"Gray. TMI." Pat said.

"Anyway, Rafael must have seen me come out of the wrong room, added two and two to make five, and suggested Pat would be interested in knowing what I'd been up to. I said he already did, and walked off."

"So he didn't actually say he wanted money to keep quiet?" Charlie asked.

"He didn't need to, sweetie. It's obvious that's what he was after." Pat said.

"You weren't even there," Gray said, and the verbal back-and-forth started up again.

"I'll get the wine," Charlie said with a smile. "Because I refuse to take sides."

But it's very interesting. Would Rafael have asked for money? Did he want the power that comes from knowing a secret? Or was he simply making trouble? And was it something he made a habit of?

They spent the rest of the meal rehearsing what Pat and Gray knew about the murder, and about Rafael and his many amours. They teased Charlie about hooking up with José Maria, trying to wheedle out the "juicy details" as Pat put it. Charlie shared only that it had been a very satisfactory encounter, and thanked them (with more booze) for taking him to the club. He kept quiet about everything to do with the murder — if they knew he'd seen the body, they would want the "juicy details" about that too. Let them keep their illusions that real life murder was as bloodless as it was on TV.

Dinner over, they moved to the bar, where a sultry young woman in impossible heels and a painted-on dress was singing cover versions of Nina Simone and Amy Winehouse. She was very good and deserved all her applause and tips.

"Another of Rafael's conquests?" Charlie asked. Pat and Gray laughed.

"Not a chance in hell. She's as queer as us. Maybe queerer. Seven out of six on the Kinsey scale."

They stayed until the bar closed, and there was no suggestion of going dancing, probably because none of them were very steady on their feet. Pat and Gray staggered in the direction of their room arm-in-arm, and Charlie wove his way unsteadily between the hedges until he found his own. He managed to get his keycard into its slot on the third attempt, so he could put the bathroom light on for a pee, then drank three glasses of water and fell into bed.

CHARLIE'S BLADDER woke him at five am. He tried to ignore it and failed. The room smelled of sweat and stale booze, so he opened the sliding door to let some fresh air in. It came with a gentle breeze and the scent of the trees. Dawn was hours away, but the birds had begun to sing in anticipation of a new day. Between the buildings, the paths were lit by dim lamps, pointing downwards — just enough light for guests to find their way, but not enough to keep anyone, or any thing awake. Charlie stepped onto his terrace. A huge silver moon hung low in the sky overhead, and he had a sudden urge to see it reflected in the pool. He didn't bother with shoes and decided that his pyjama pants were decent — if anyone was looking.

The brick path was sharp under his bare feet after the smoothness of the tiles on his terrace and in his room. The side of the pool, when he reached it, was made from poured concrete, rougher than the tiles, but not as sharp as the bricks. His feet enjoyed the texture as he walked around the edge of the water. The moon was bright enough to cast grey shadows from the furled umbrellas and sun beds in their rows. The poolside bar was closed and shuttered, but there were lights within the hotel proper, and the only sounds were bird song and susurration in the breeze. The "waterfall" running over black lava stones had been switched off and was in deep shadow; the stones absorbing the light from the moon, leaving the pool as still as a mirror. He wanted a pebble to throw. Just one, to disturb the scene, to break the reflection. He wanted to watch the moon ripple outwards. But the area around the pool was pristine.

Charlie made his way towards the pile of rocks making up the "waterfall". Surely there would be a tiny stone hidden among the mortared fakery?

He never found out. Because the silent waterfall was concealing something else. A person floating face down in the water.

Chapter 7

Charlie recognised death when he saw it, but he dragged the body from the water anyway. It was Marita, and she was much too cold for there to be any possibility of life returning.

He ran to the hotel, and up the stairs to the reception desk, where a lone woman sat reading a magazine. There was no sign of anyone else.

"A woman is dead in the swimming pool," he gasped, "call the police."

The receptionist, whose name tag read "Carmela," stared at Charlie, taking in his soaked pyjama trousers, and the water dripping from his body. She made no attempt to use the phone.

"Dead body in the pool," he said again. "Call the police. Policia. Do it! Do it now!"

Slowly she reacted, flicking nervous glances at Charlie as she spoke. When she finished, he said: "Are they coming?" She nodded. "I'll wait by the pool," Charlie said, "to show them where to go." The receptionist said nothing, and he went back downstairs, dripping onto the tiled floor. The air that had felt warm when he left his room now seemed cold on his wet skin. He noticed that the birds had stopped singing.

Within minutes, the first police cars arrived. Two uniforms and the chief inspector from this morning.

"We meet again, Señor Rees," he said.

Over his shoulder, Charlie saw another police officer arrive. It was José Maria, face twisted with horror.

FOR THE SECOND time in twenty-four hours, Charlie faced José Maria's boss in the seating area of his hotel room.

"You decided to go for a walk in the middle of the night? And found a dead body? The second one today?"

Charlie shrugged miserably. *He* wouldn't have believed it either.

"I have investigated *you* Señor Rees — Detective Sergeant Rees. Impress me. Detect. What is going on? Tell me why you keep finding bodies."

No pressure then.

Charlie cleared his throat, wishing he had done more than change his wet pyjamas for yesterday's jeans and a hoodie. He wanted the confidence of his best suit, to have had a shave, and ideally four cups of coffee.

"Well," he began, "it can't have been anything to do with José Maria. Even if you don't believe that he was with me all last night, he was working tonight."

"Working alone, Detective Sergeant Rees. And Perez has the best motive of anyone involved in this mess."

"Huh?" Charlie was as sure as he could be that he hadn't been having sex with a murderer, but he was disconcerted by the certainty in the policeman's tone.

"Many people do not approve of gays. You know this. There are people who think José Maria should not be a police officer."

Charlie nodded. "You think Rafael was making trouble? Threatening José Maria, maybe even blackmailing him?"

"You don't?"

"Making trouble seems to have been Rafael's thing. That and seducing every woman he could. I know he was seen kissing Elisa, and if he had loved her and left her, then Marita would have been angry with him. And she bought a knife."

"She had a history of violence. With knives. Went to prison for it. You didn't know that?"

"Psychiatric hospital was what I heard," Charlie said.

"That too," the detective replied.

"So there's your answer. It's very sad. Overprotective mother. Mental illness."

"Detective Sergeant Rees … you can't even convince yourself. You are quite right that Marita did buy a knife. She took it home, unwrapped it and used it to chop vegetables. We found it in her kitchen with the packaging in her bin. But Marita is dead."

"Suicide?"

"You don't believe that any more than I do."

That was true. Charlie was sure that Marita had been murdered, and by the same person who had murdered Rafael. But he wasn't ready to believe it was José Maria. Not yet. He thought of Marita and what she had said — cried — when he had taken her to sit down away from the body. *I saw … I saw* … What had Marita seen?

"Marita saw something in that room, not just Rafael's body. Something else. Something that had meaning to her." Charlie said.

"Something that led to her murder?"

"Perhaps. Or something that told her who else had been in the room."

Charlie closed his eyes and visualised the scene. All the blood. The body. The knife. *The knife.*

"Marita bought a knife. Why? Surely she already had a knife to chop vegetables?" Charlie said. "Unless someone had used her knife to murder Rafael. Someone who had been ill-treated by Rafael, who had thought his kisses meant something more than they did?"

"Elisa? No. Elisa knew Rafael couldn't be trusted. Everyone on the island knew that. Elisa wouldn't kill her own mother. No, my friend."

Charlie knew well that people killed their own parents. If Elisa wanted to cut the apron strings, to stand on her own feet, to make something with attractive bad boy Rafael. She could have told herself he would change. He ran these arguments past his companion.

"Everything you say is possible, Detective Sergeant Rees. But do you not remember Elisa's behaviour this morning? *What have you done to my mother?* Elisa loved her mother as much as Marita loved her. I'm sure of it."

Silence fell. The sun was shining through the voile curtains. It was the fourth day of Charlie's holiday, and he was spending it trying to convince this man that his lover hadn't murdered two people. He visualised the crime scene again; saw José Maria standing in the charnel-house doorway and leaving bloody footprints on the tiled floor of the hall. Did the blood come from stepping on that bloodied towel, or had it come from earlier, while Charlie had been sleeping? Were José Maria's feet what Marita had seen?

Outside, he could hear the housekeeping staff wheeling their trollies full of clean towels along the brick paths, calling out to one another in rapid Spanish. Someone was using a leaf blower, or a hedge trimmer — some kind of machine that buzzed quietly but persistently. The scent of the tamarisk trees drifted into the room.

No. José Maria had been disgusted by the blood on his feet. Marita had not been afraid of him, as she surely would have been if she thought José Maria was the killer. There must be something else.

. . .

BLOOD. Blood everywhere. Soaking the white bedcovers, splashed on the patterned headboard, blood on the bedside table, coating a phone, a wallet and a hotel keycard, blood in Rorschach blots on the floor. A bloody towel lay on the tiles like a doormat. In the middle of it all, on the bed, the body of a naked man, both arms covered in tattoos. And blood.

YOUR BOYFRIEND HAS A CHILD. A child he wants to keep contact with. When a marriage breaks down, people aren't reasonable. They look for ways to make themselves look like the "injured party" …

A FEW WEEKS AGO, I would have said Rafael was fucking my wife …

"WAS the key card in its slot by the door in Rafael's room?" Charlie asked.

The detective nodded.

"Then whose was the card on the bedside table? Rafael didn't need two cards. Who could make a card to any room in the hotel? Someone who has as much to lose as José Maria. You say José Maria was working on his own tonight. So was Carmela."

The silence fell again, Charlie hoping that he'd found the answer, the chief inspector weighing his words.

"You make a convincing case, my friend. If you are right, we should be able to prove it. We can find out where Officer Perez's car went last night and what time Señor Perez used her computer. But you have done enough. Enjoy your holiday. Visit the beach. Swim in the pool. Get a tan. Then go home. Come back for the trial." He stood up, held out his hand to be shaken, and left.

. . .

CHARLIE SLEPT for the rest of the day, going early for dinner to avoid Pat and Gray. He settled down on the sofa in his suite to read his book. When he realised he was reading the same page for the third time, and still hadn't taken it in, he gave up and stared at the palm tree by his little terrace. *Had* he been sleeping with a murderer?

Chapter 8

Mental images and snippets of memory competed for Charlie's attention. José Maria freezing in place when Charlie said he was a police officer. Carmela's sluggish reaction to Charlie's report of a body in the pool. The state of the Perez marriage. The keycards. Seduction. Alibis. Shared childhoods in a small community. He shook his head. He had to let it go. Enjoy the last few days of sunshine and get back to work. Go to the bar and let Pat and Gray buy him a couple of drinks.

And maybe ask them a few questions.

THE TWO OLDER MEN FELL ON Charlie like a pride of lions finding an unaccompanied antelope at the waterhole. They wanted all the details of Marita's death, the discovery of her body, the police investigation, who the suspects were, and how Charlie was coping with being caught in the middle of it all. He did his best to answer their questions without adding fuel to the flames of island and hotel gossip. When he could, he inserted his own inquiries.

"Had you met José Maria before? Did you know him well?"

"Sure," Pat said. "Seen him around the club a few times. Don't think we'd ever spoken to him."

"We're much too old for a hottie like him." Gray added with a wink.

"But he'd have recognised you?"

"Sweetie, *everyone* knows us."

"As in, knows which hotel you stay at?" Charlie asked.

"I suppose so. We always stay here, and we visit a lot. Why?" Pat said.

Which was exactly the question Charlie didn't want to answer. Because if José Maria had known who Pat and Gray were, and where they were staying, had he deliberately hooked up with Charlie to get access to the hotel? Had he known that Rafael would be there? But Charlie didn't believe it. José Maria would have had to know which room Rafael was in, before trying to seduce Charlie. It was too complicated to be likely.

Unless it was a mixture of intent and coincidence. Could José Maria have caught sight of Rafael while he and Charlie were winding their drunken way back to Charlie's room? In which case, did he just happen to have a knife? No, it still didn't add up.

"Charlie? Sweetie? Are you still with us?" Pat was smiling and holding up his empty glass.

"Oh. Sorry, yes, please. I was miles away."

"You OK?" Gray asked when Pat had gone to the bar.

Charlie assured him that all was well, and resolved to keep quiet about José Maria. Because it couldn't have been him. No way.

When the bar closed, Charlie strolled across the hotel grounds with Pat and Gray until they arrived at the turnoff for their room. Charlie kept going in the direction of his own room, then when Pat and Gray were out of sight, turned round and walked back towards the pool. He found a sun bed in a quiet spot and sat down to wait.

Once the bar had emptied, and the hotel was quiet, Charlie stood up, stretched and made his way to reception. A woman sat on a high stool behind the desk, entering something from slips of paper into her computer. She looked up and smiled with genuine friendliness.

"Hi," Charlie said. "I'm really sorry, but I can't find my keycard to get back into my room. I think I must have dropped it somewhere." He pulled his best Mr-Bean-is-confused face. "I'm such a half-wit. I can't seem to keep these things in my pockets, no matter how hard I try."

"I can make you another card. What is your room number, please?"

Charlie extended a hand over the counter. "Charlie Rees. Seven seven three. Look. I have the little card you gave me to show at mealtimes." He produced the now rather battered piece of cardboard with his room number and his 'fully inclusive' status. She took the card and started typing.

"I'm sorry to disturb you. You were busy." Charlie said.

The woman laughed. "It's fine. The job is necessary, but it's dull." She stood up and opened a drawer. Charlie saw it was full of cash as well as a stack of keycards.

"Um, it's none of my business," Charlie said, "but well, I'm a police detective in the UK, and I don't think you should have all that cash on display when you're on your own at night."

The receptionist blushed, grabbed a keycard, and closed the drawer.

Charlie took a step back and held up his hands. "Sorry. Don't mean to cause trouble. I can't help thinking like a police officer. I'm sure you aren't on your own."

She smiled. "No trouble. We may be alone, but it is quite safe. I'll make you a new key."

"Thank you." He left a pause. "I was chatting to one of your colleagues — Carmela — yesterday. I thought she might be here tonight." It felt clumsy and the receptionist would peg him as a creep as well as an idiot. The kind of man to pretend to lose his key so that he could chat up a woman. Charlie blushed, which probably confirmed her suspicions.

"Carmela … no longer works here," the receptionist said. "Here is your new key. I'm afraid we will have to charge you twenty-five euros if you lose it again." She smiled, though the friendliness had gone.

"Is Carmela working in a different hotel?" Now she would definitely have him in the creep category, but her answer made him think she hadn't fallen for any of it.

"If you really are a policía, señor Rees, then you will know exactly where Carmela Perez is."

I am, and thanks to you, I can make a good guess.

Chapter 9

Charlie couldn't sleep; his mind unable to let go of the murders. He had no method of contacting José Maria, or the chief inspector, even if he wanted to. He wasn't sure that he did. But he did want to know more about the Perez marital dispute. Could one of them have murdered two people to give themselves an advantage in the divorce? It had made sense when he was talking to the chief inspector, but in the cold light of day, or rather night, it seemed like a thin motive. Except the motive only had to be meaningful to the murderer, and not to anyone else.

The wise detective looks at means and opportunities.

Carmela Perez was alone on the reception desk at the time of both murders. She could get access to Raphael's room and no one would question her presence anywhere on the site. The knife was a long-bladed kitchen knife. The kind of thing anyone could have. But possessing the knife and using it to kill a living person were two different things. Was Carmela angry enough, or cold-blooded enough? Or had she felt in danger from Rafael? Rafael was a fit young man and surely not easy to overpower. Charlie had no sense of how tall or strong Carmela was — he'd only seen her sitting on a stool behind the reception desk. But regardless of her size and strength, did she have the *will* to stab a man she had slept with?

Could she have murdered Marita? Marita was tiny, barely five feet tall and thin with it. But again, merely because Carmela could have physically carried out the murder, didn't mean she had the guts to do it.

José Maria was a police officer. His job included getting physical; he was trained to use a weapon, to defend himself against violence, to use violence in pursuit of law and order. It was far less of a stretch to imagine José Maria wielding a knife.

For a moment, Charlie flirted with the idea of a random stranger, or a passing psychopath. He re-examined Marita as the murderer of Raphael. She had bought a new knife and used it for chopping veg. But she could have used a knife from the hotel kitchens, or another knife from her own kitchen.

Round and round went the thoughts, reaching no conclusions. Charlie turned the light on and tried to read, but Jack Reacher was no help, and he couldn't concentrate on the words. He needed more information, and he doubted he would get it from the police. He decided to visit Andres at the beachside bar. Maybe he could at least learn more about the people in the case. Decision made, he finally slept.

THE NEXT MORNING, Charlie was at the little bar before it opened. Andres gave him a curious look before the light dawned.

"Charlie, right? José Maria's friend."

Charlie nodded. "Can I talk to you about José Maria? Just for a minute before you get busy?"

"You want to talk about José Maria? Sure. Sit down. Do you want coffee?" Andres walked towards a pile of folded chairs, picked one up, put it down again, and finally unfolded it next to one of the tables. Then he unlocked the door and disappeared inside. A few minutes later, he returned with two coffees in cardboard cups, put them on the table and collected another chair for himself.

"What about José Maria?" Andres asked.

Charlie had already decided that honesty was the best policy. He had two more days to find out what he could — hopefully to clear José Maria of any involvement.

"I'm a police officer—a detective—at home. José Maria's boss thinks he did the murders. I don't. But I can't prove it."

Andres rubbed his neck. "Why does he think that?"

Charlie had expected an outraged denial that José Maria could have been involved. They were supposed to have been friends since childhood, after all. It was an interesting reaction.

"That maybe Rafael was blackmailing him. Threatening to tell his wife about his affairs with other men, so he could lose contact with his child."

Andres leaned forward, pushing the cardboard cup of coffee to one side. "Rafael was probably threatening them both, because he was a turd. The rest is bullshit."

"Because José Maria's wife already knew?"

"Because she doesn't *care*. They got married because Carmela got pregnant, and has a lot of nasty brothers. She thought José Maria was a better prospect than all the other men she'd been fucking. Which obviously he is, or will be once he stops pretending to be a cop. The brothers did the rest. Then the two of them carried on as if there was no marriage. Clubs, bars, affairs. The baby spends his time with his grandmother — Carmela's mother. They are my friends, but ..." Andres shook his head. "They are wild."

A young couple stopped at their table. "Can we get a drink?" the young man asked.

Andres pushed his chair back. "I have to go," he said to Charlie.

Charlie picked up his coffee and took it down to the

beach, sitting on the sand and leaning his back against a black boulder. There were no waves to speak of, but even so, it was soothing staring at the sea, letting his mind drift.

José Maria had lied about his relationship with his wife, and about what she knew. Charlie wondered what else he'd been lying about, and who else had been lying. Something José Maria had said came back to him with new significance. He drank the last of his coffee, crumpled the cup and stood up. There was no sign of Andres outside the bar, so Charlie went inside. Andres was behind the counter, working a complicated coffee machine.

"One last thing," he said. "Why did you say José Maria is playing at being a cop?"

"Because his family own half the island. They don't like Carmela and José Maria won't go crawling back to beg forgiveness for getting her pregnant."

"But he could? Ask for forgiveness, I mean."

"You should ask him. I've said enough."

CHARLIE WALKED BACK to the hotel as the pieces of the case rearranged themselves in his mind to form a clear and perfect solution. It made him feel sick.

Chapter 10

Now he was sure about what had happened, Charlie found he was happy to leave it to the island police. They had the resources to check on José Maria's and Carmela's movements. The police would have access to the post mortem results on the two victims, and the results of all the forensic investigations. Most important, they would live with the results. He would go home and try to forget. If they called him as a witness, he would turn up and say what he had seen and done. He could spend his last day by the pool.

Time to put on the last pair of clean shorts.

The knock at the door startled him. He quickly pulled his shorts on and went to open it, expecting the housekeeper with her trolley and buckets. His "holà" turned into an "oof" as he was pushed backwards into the room.

José Maria slammed the door behind him and levelled his gun at Charlie's chest. He was wearing his navy blue island police uniform. His lips were a tight, thin line, and his eyes were cold.

"I liked you Charlie. I liked sex with you. A bit of fun. That's what it should have been."

Charlie told himself that José Maria wouldn't shoot. Logically, it made no sense — the bullet would identify the gun, and the gun would be traced to José Maria. But his body didn't recognise the logic. His body was terrified. Sweat turned to ice on his face. His knees buckled. He sat down hard on the bed.

"You lied to me," he said, because that was the thing uppermost in his mind. Not, *you and your wife murdered two people.*

"I didn't lie. You asked the wrong questions."

"Your boss knows it was you. But my alibi will stand up in court. Raphael was a blackmailer. Everyone hates blackmailers. With a good lawyer, you can get away with this. But if you shoot me, all bets are off."

José Maria took a step forward.

Too close. Rookie mistake.

"Maybe I don't want your alibi. Maybe I won't be going to court. Maybe I won't be here."

Make conversation.

"You're leaving? Taking Carmela?"

"That bitch? No chance. Telling Raphael everything, showing off, bragging about the money we were going to get from my family. Like I was going to give her any."

"She helped you with the murders."

He's relaxing. Keep talking.

"I think maybe she killed Marita, or was that you as well?"

"Does it matter?" José Maria swayed on his feet. Charlie thought he looked exhausted. This murdering lark must take it out of a person. He couldn't help a smile. A hysterical, manic smile. The sort of smile he'd seen on the faces of some bereaved people as if the body wasn't sure about what emotion to show, and the wrong one was better than none at all. José Maria swayed again, backwards, away from the man smiling at a gun, and Charlie jumped.

He slammed into José Maria, knocking him off his feet. Charlie's weight kept them both on the floor, José Maria pinned beneath him, unable to move his gun hand from under

Charlie's knee. But his finger was on the trigger, and his body was thrashing to escape. Unless Charlie did something, José Maria would wriggle his hand free and shoot him. But anything he did would give José Maria his chance.

Fuck.

Charlie bit José Maria's ear as hard as he could, and then he started yelling into his face to break his focus.

Except José Maria's job was dealing with drunks. Drunks who yelled and bit. What would have shocked a civilian had no effect. Charlie felt the hand with the gun moving, no matter how hard he pushed his knee onto it.

I am NOT letting him shoot me.

He kept yelling. José Maria kept squirming. Charlie lifted his head and brought his forehead as down hard as he could on José Maria's nose. There wasn't enough force to break bones, but there was plenty of blood. So he did it again, and this time he felt something break. And kept yelling, calling for help and the police. José Maria was blinded by his own blood, but he didn't need to see to pull the trigger. All he needed was a tiny bit of wiggle room. Charlie was losing the ability to keep stop him getting it.

There was a loud pounding on the door, and the click of a key card in the lock. Charlie gasped with relief, and that was the opening José Maria wanted. Before Charlie could react, José Maria had thrown him off and pressed the gun to Charlie's head.

Three uniformed officers burst through the door, and behind them, the chief inspector.

"Back off or I kill him," José Maria said. "Get out!"

The three uniforms stepped back, but Charlie saw they all had their guns out.

"You too, Jefe," José Maria said, but the chief inspector didn't move.

"This is over now, Officer Perez." He took a step towards

them. Charlie saw that he, too, had a gun in his hand. He took another step. He was now only a yard away.

"Back off, Jefe. I'll kill him." Charlie felt the faintest tremble from the gun pressed to his head. He tensed, his shoulders stiffening, his breath shallow and his heart painful in his chest. A sharp pain stabbed into his neck as he strained to lean away from the gun. He smelled sweat, his own and José Maria's. There was no noise except for the sound of breathing. The air was still, each molecule in suspense, waiting … Charlie's breath hurt.

The chief inspector took the final step. Without speaking, he lifted his hand, grasped José Maria's wrist and lowered the gun from Charlie's head.

"Good choice, Officer Perez," he said, and just as calmly took the gun from José Maria. He looked over his shoulder, and jerked his head. The uniformed officers came in, handcuffed José Maria, and led him away.

"Sit down, Señor Rees."

Charlie didn't so much sit down, as collapse onto the bed, suddenly cold and shaking. The chief inspector stood and looked down at him.

"You're going to remind me that I should have left it alone," Charlie said.

"For your sake, yes. For us? You have made our job easier, so no."

"They were in it together? Carmela and José Maria. Both being blackmailed by Raphael?" Charlie asked.

"All the evidence points that way," the chief inspector replied. "Carmela has been, shall we say, forthcoming. Raphael was threatening to tell José Maria's parents about their lifestyle, just as the two of them were planning to try for reconciliation. There is a lot of money at stake. It is very sad." The chief inspector put his hand on Charlie's shoulder. "This is a peaceful place. Don't judge us by what has happened this week."

"I won't. But, sir," Charlie used the honorific without conscious thought, "how did you know José Maria would give you the gun?"

"I didn't. But if he hadn't, I'm sure you would have kicked his legs out from underneath him when he looked at me. I had every faith in you, Señor Rees." The chief inspector shrugged and smiled. With a squeeze of Charlie's shoulder, he was gone.

Chapter 11

Charlie needed company and alcohol, so he went in search of Pat and Gray. He found them by the pool, stretched out on sun beds, 'specials' in hand. He sat down next to Pat with a 'special' of his own.

"Sweetie, what on Earth has been going on? We are hearing terrible stories of police officers waving guns, and one of their number dragged away in handcuffs."

"That's what happened," Charlie said. "The officer in handcuffs was José Maria. He killed Rafael and Marita." Charlie knew whatever he said to Pat and Gray would be shared with everyone they met, but he was leaving the next day, and anyway he needed to talk, if only to get things clear in his head.

Pat clapped a hand to his mouth. "Oh. My. God. José Maria killed two people? But he was so good looking."

Charlie snorted with laughter, sending his drink spraying over his shirt. He dabbed at it with a paper napkin.

"Take it off and get some rays," Gray said.

"Let him ogle you more like," Pat said. "Now tell us about these murders before I die of curiosity."

Charlie took his shirt off with a grin. The sun felt delicious on his skin. He snagged the bottle of sun cream from underneath Pat's lounger.

"May I?"

"Help yourself, sweetie. Just say if you need a hand rubbing it in."

"So," he said when he had finished protecting his pale skin, "José Maria comes from a very religious, very wealthy family. They didn't approve of Carmela, but she got pregnant and they got married. Carm …"

"But he's *gay*." Pat interrupted.

"Won't be the first time a gay man has got a girl pregnant," Gray said drily.

"Well, *I've* never seen him with a girl," Pat said.

Gray opened his mouth to respond, but Charlie got in first.

"I don't know if José Maria is bi, or if Carmela was a beard. But they got married and had a baby and a big row with José Maria's parents. José Maria got the job with the police to prove he didn't need his parents' money. And now I'm guessing a bit, but I think Carmela wanted a better life than their salaries provided. They were planning a reconciliation."

"Where does Raphael come in?" Pat asked.

"If you let him finish, maybe you'd find out," Gray said. "I've a good mind to send you for drinks while I hear the rest of the story. In peace."

"I'll get the drinks," Charlie said. He stood up and walked over to the bar to the sound of *now look what you've done*, and *we'll stop interrupting then*. When he got back, the two men were sitting like two little birds waiting to be fed.

"Raphael came in because he was, as Pat deduced, a blackmailer." Pat squeaked as Gray clamped his hand over his husband's mouth.

"It seems," Charlie went on, "that José Maria and Carmela lived a pretty wild life. As we know, José Maria went to gay bars and picked up men, and Carmela had lovers of her own. Carmela's mother looked after the baby. One of Carmela's lovers was Raphael. Perhaps she told him about their attempt to reconcile with José Maria's parents. Perhaps he guessed. Either way, he knew that there would be no reconciliation if the Perez seniors found out about the gay bars and assorted lovers. So he tried to blackmail them, and they killed him for it."

Gray still had a hand covering Pat's mouth. "One question," he said, "how did you guess?"

Charlie didn't like to think of detective work as *guessing*, but that wasn't important. Or not very.

"I didn't want it to be José Maria," he shrugged, "because, well, you know why. I decided it had to be Carmela. She was working alone when both the murders occurred, she had access to the whole hotel, she knew where Raphael was staying because she was going to meet him there. But I couldn't imagine her stabbing a man to death. Or killing Marita and leaving her body in the pool. On the other hand, I *could* imagine José Maria killing two people. Not because he seemed violent, but because he's in a violent job. He works nights keeping the peace in a resort where there is drinking, and probably drugs. He has to break up fights and get people off the streets who don't want to go. Physical stuff."

Charlie took a drink and looked up. Pat and Gray had identical fascinated expressions—eyes like chapel hat pegs, his mother would have said—and he noticed they were holding hands so tightly that the skin on their knuckles had turned white.

"I could believe that José Maria had left me asleep and gone to murder Raphael, only how did he know where Raphael was? How did he get hold of a knife, plastic gloves, a shower hat, or a keycard to the room? I decided he couldn't have done it. He as good as told me his parents were rich, and that they didn't know he had sex with men, but he also told me he and Carmela didn't get on. This morning I found out that wasn't true. José Maria and Carmela may not have had a traditional marriage, but it worked for them. I also found out about the proposed reconciliation, and it all fell into place. Neither one could have done the murders alone, but together, it was easy."

Charlie sighed. It was going to take a long time to forget that he had sex with a murderer, and liked it. He had been comprehensively used and lied to because he'd fallen for a pretty face, a good body, and a sexy accent. For the first time he understood how so many people fell for scammers promising love or wealth. The chief inspector had tried to warn him, and that made it worse; made him feel more foolish. He had blundered about in a foreign country, thinking he knew what he was doing, and the result was that he almost got killed. Those thoughts would remain unshared.

"So, anyway, José Maria came to my room, and the police were following and they arrested him. I think Carmela had already confessed. That's it really."

"You're so clever," Pat said, patting Charlie's arm. "You should be a detective."

TWO DAYS LATER, Charlie walked into the police station in the small Welsh town where he lived. His chief inspector gave him a big smile.

"Had a nice relaxing holiday, Charlie-boy? You've gone a funny colour anyway."

"Sunshine does that, boss."

"I wouldn't know. Haven't seen any round here. Now then, work. Nothing interesting. No murders or mayhem. Thefts of farm machinery are as good as it gets."

Charlie thought that sounded perfect.

I HOPE you enjoyed meeting Charlie away from the usual Melin Tywyll gang. If you want to know what happens next, you can pre-order here

Acknowledgments

Thanks are due to Lou and Austin, who provided their usual encouragement, as well as the necessary words of criticism. I am lucky to have two such excellent friends.

I'm not going to name the fabulous hotel on Lanzarote, where I stayed while writing this story. Suffice it to say that I had a wonderful time. The sun shone. The staff were universally helpful, the other guests were friendly and the facilities delightful. I'd also like to thank everyone who helped carry my bags, provided service with a smile, and rescued me from the M4 when the exhaust fell off my vehicle. An eventful journey.

Thanks also to Layla Ndn, PA extraordinaire, and to SF for keeping me, mostly, sane.

About the Author

Ripley Hayes lives in rural Wales, where most of her stories are based. She writes mysteries one reviewer compared to Ruth Rendell; a compliment she hopes is justified. Her characters are usually gay, and they often have to solve their cases while dealing with the challenge that is life. Sometimes they fall in love.

She is frequently distracted by a certain dog, who likes to keep a poor author from getting too comfortable.

Her website is at ripleyhayes.com

You can find her on Facebook at Ripley and co

Also by Ripley Hayes

Daniel Owen Books

1: Undermined

2: Dark Water

3: Leavings

4: A Man

5: Too Many Fires

6: An Allotment of Time

7. A Teachable Moment

Peter Tudor and Lorne Stewart Cosy Mysteries

1: No Accident in Abergwyn: 2nd edition available

2: No Friends in Abergwyn

Teema Crowe

Badly Served

Paul Qayf

Secret State: Enemy

Printed in Great Britain
by Amazon